59444
Ants Don't Catch Flying Sau

P9-DCO-175

Trina Wiebe
AR B.L.: 4.2
Points: 2.0

Ants Don't Catch Flying Saucers

by Trina Wiebe

Illustrations
by Marisol Sarrazin

Lobster Press™

Published by Lobster Press™
1620 Sherbrooke Street West, Suites C & D
Montréal, Québec   H3H 1C9
Tel. (514) 904-1100 • Fax (514) 904-1101 • www.lobsterpress.com

Publisher: Alison Fripp
Editor: Jane Pavanel
Cover design: Marielle Maheu
Layout and design: Genviève Mayers & Allison Larin

Distributed in the United States by: Distributed in Canada by:
Advanced Global Distribution Services   Raincoast Books
5880 Oberlin Drive   9050 Shaughnessey Street
San Diego, CA 92121   Vancouver, BC   V6P 6E5

We acknowledge the financial support of the Government of Canada through the
Book Publishing Industry Development Program (BPIDP) for our publishing activities.

The Canada Council   Le Conseil des Arts
for the Arts   du Canada

We acknowledge the support of the Canada
Council for the Arts for our publishing program.

National Library of Canada Cataloguing in Publication Data
Wiebe, Trina, 1970-
     Ants don't catch flying saucers

(Abby and Tess, pet-sitters; 5)
ISBN 1-894222-31-8

     I. Sarrazin, Marisol, 1965- II. Series: Wiebe, Trina, 1970-.
Abby and Tess, pet-sitters ; 5.

PS8595.I358A88 2001   jC813'.6   C2001-900209-2
PZ7.W6349An 2001

Printed and bound in Canada

Contents

To Aubrey, Kara and Gerard — this one's for you!
– T.W.

1 Dirk the Jerk

"Do you see our names?" asked Abby, pushing through the crowd of kids. "Are we on the same team?"

Rachel stood on her tiptoes and strained to see the notice that was tacked to the classroom bulletin board. "I don't know, I can't see yet."

Abby spotted an opening and darted forward. She found herself right in front of the notice. The words "Crazy Olympics" were written across the top in bold red letters.

It gave Abby a thrill just to read them. Everyone in Mrs. Hernandez's fifth grade class had been waiting all year for this. There would be games, contests and a party, and best of all, a whole afternoon with no schoolwork!

Abby scanned the list of teams. Written under each team name were the names of four or five students. It would be so cool if she and Rachel were together.

"Here you are," she cried. She underlined the words with her finger. "Fantastic French Fries . . . Rachel Katz."

Rachel giggled. The class had chosen the team names the week before. "What about you?"

Abby's shoulders slumped. "I'm not here." She searched some more. "Oh no," she groaned. Not only wasn't she on Rachel's team, she was on Dirk Kaefermann's team. Dirk was the most irritating boy in the class. He was always teasing her, or trying to scare her with bugs he'd collected on the playground, like spiders and ants and caterpillars. Ugh. Abby shuddered just thinking about it.

"I'm a Giggling Grayhound," she said glumly.

Her little sister, Tess, would have been thrilled to be a Giggling Grayhound. Tess loved dogs. She loved them so much that she acted like one most of the time. She was always scratching at the apartment door when she wanted out, or barking at strangers they passed

2

on the street.

Abby loved all animals, which was why she was determined to be a veterinarian when she grew up. Normally, she would have been proud to call herself a Giggling Grayhound, but not if it meant being on the same team as Dirk.

"Oh well," said Rachel, "it'll still be fun."

Rachel was right. The events in the Crazy Olympics would be a blast. Mrs. Hernandez had organized fruit bowling, a flying saucer relay, a three-legged speed-skating race, and a backwards obstacle course. Afterwards there would be a big party in their classroom with music and lots of food. If only she could have been a Fantastic French Fry.

Someone pushed Abby and she stumbled forward, bumping into the wall.

"Out of my way, dweeb!"

Abby didn't turn around. There was no mistaking that annoying, squeaky voice. Besides, Dirk bumped into her all the time. Abby ignored him and went back to her seat. She didn't want him to see how angry he made her. Maybe one of these days he'd give up and find someone else to bug.

Dirk and his friends shoved and elbowed each other in front of the bulletin board. The noise level rose higher and higher as they discovered what teams they were on.

"Oh, man! What a lousy team," Dirk complained loud enough for everyone to hear. "We're going to lose for sure."

"Don't listen to him," said Rachel, joining Abby at her desk. "He's totally immature."

"I know," said Abby. She glared across the room at Dirk and his buddies. The Crazy Olympics were a week away, which meant the Giggling Grayhounds would be stuck together for three whole gym classes. She wasn't sure she could stand being on the same team as Dirk for that long.

"We should be called the Laughing Losers, not the Giggling Grayhounds," Dirk continued. "Hey, we need a loser leader. I nominate Abby."

Abby felt her face go hot. Why wouldn't

Dirk leave her alone? Mom said boys teased girls they secretly liked, but Mom was obviously wrong. The only thing Dirk liked was making Abby feel stupid.

"My name is Abby," said Dirk in a high voice. He flipped back an imaginary lock of hair. "I'm a big loser."

His friends snickered as he took a few mincing steps forward, hands on hips. Soon the whole class was laughing at his Abby impression.

Abby couldn't stand it anymore. "Why don't you grow up?" she snapped.

Dirk immediately brought his hand to his forehead in a military salute. "Aye, aye, Captain Loser!" His friends copied him.

"Don't let them get to you," whispered Rachel. She grabbed Abby's arm and tried to turn her away. "They just want to make you mad."

But Abby wasn't mad. She was furious! A hush fell over the room as she marched up to Dirk. She narrowed her eyes and brought her nose close to his. "Why don't you leave me alone? Why do you have to be such a . . . such a . . . JERK!"

"Yeah," added Rachel. "Dirk the jerk."

The class cracked up again, but this time they weren't laughing at Abby. Startled into silence, Dirk stared at Abby for a moment. She was surprised to see a hurt look in his eyes. Then he glanced away. When he met her gaze again, the hurt look was gone and in its place was his usual mocking expression.

"Can't you take a joke?" he smirked. He turned to his buddies just as Mrs. Hernandez walked through the door. "Some people have no sense of humor."

Abby felt a twinge of guilt, but pushed it aside. She was probably mistaken about the wounded look she'd just seen. Dirk called her names all the time. Why would he care if she did the same thing to him?

2 Tryouts

"Tweeeet!"

Miss Q, the gym teacher, blew a sharp blast on her whistle. Her last name was really Qitsualik, but everyone called her Miss Q. Her long black hair was drawn into a high ponytail and she wore stretchy athletic pants with stripes up the sides. The students gathered around her, whispering and laughing.

"Does everyone know which team they're on?" she asked, consulting her clipboard.

The whole class answered at once.

"Hiccuping Hyenas!"

"Marvelous Marshmallows!"

"Fantastic French Fries," cried a frizzy-haired girl named Autumn.

"Giggling Grayhounds," Zachary and Dirk shouted in unison.

Miss Q held her hand in the air, signaling for quiet. "Okay, good. We've got one week to practice. I realize our Crazy Olympics are a little different from the true Olympic Games, but we're still athletes, and all athletes have to train for their events. Training! Practice! Team-work!"

The gym exploded with clapping and cheering.

Miss Q blew the whistle again. When she had the students' attention, she continued.

"Remember, each event earns points for your team. The team with the most points wins. It's a group effort, people, so let's work together. Four teams, four events, four stations set up around the gym. We'll switch every 15 minutes. Let the training begin!"

Running shoes squeaked on the gymnasium floor as the kids raced to form their teams. Abby's steps were much slower than everyone else's. She glanced at the Fantastic French Fries and tried to catch Rachel's eye, but Rachel was talking to Autumn and didn't notice. Reluctantly, Abby kept walking.

Five Giggling Grayhounds stood under the basketball hoop at the far end of the gym.

There was Dirk, of course, and his best friend Zachary, plus the Cooper twins, Dana and Dinah, and a quiet boy named Melvin. Abby could hear Dirk's voice even before she joined the group.

"Okay, listen up. This is what we're going to do . . ."

"Who made him the boss?" muttered Abby crossly.

Dirk turned to her. "Did you say something, Captain Loser?"

Abby clenched her fists and shoved them into her pockets. "Why do you get to decide everything?"

Dirk shrugged. "We need to find out who's best at what, right?"

"Yeah," said Zachary. "Don't you want to win?"

"Sure," Abby said. "But Dirk's giving orders like he's the one in charge, when he's not."

Dinah stepped forward. "He's only trying to organize the team," she told Abby. "Miss Q said we need to work together."

Dana and Melvin nodded. Behind them, Dirk grinned and stuck out his tongue at Abby.

Abby resisted the urge to say something nasty. "Fine. Let's just get started."

The Giggling Grayhounds spent the rest of gym class going from station to station, deciding who would compete in which event. They started with the three-legged speed-skating race.

Abby and Melvin stood side by side, their two inside legs tied together with strips of cotton. Dana and Dinah had paired off, and so had Dirk and Zachary.

Melvin straightened the square of carpeting under their middle "leg." The trick was to slide the carpet across the gym floor without losing their balance.

Easier said than done, thought Abby. She liked Melvin, but everyone knew he couldn't walk down the hallway without tripping over his own feet.

"Ready?" Abby asked him.

"Ready as I'll ever be," he said with a nervous laugh.

"Go!" shouted Dirk.

Abby and Melvin lurched forward. Unfortunately, their "skate" stayed behind. They backtracked as fast as they could, a clumsy tangle of arms and legs. By the time they retrieved the carpet and started again, Dana and Dinah had swooshed across the finish line.

"Switch," barked Miss Q.

Next was the bowling event. Melvin turned out to be surprisingly talented with fruit. His cantaloupe whizzed across the floor and sent the foam pins flying. Abby's grapefruit, on the other hand, rolled into the equipment closet, and Dirk's honeydew melon smacked into the wall and split open.

"Tweeeet," screeched Miss Q's whistle. "Switch!"

The next stop was the backwards obstacle course. Only Abby, Dirk and Zachary were left without an event.

"That settles it," said Abby. She'd seen

Dirk and Zachary tossing a saucer around at recess and they were pretty good. "You guys do the flying saucer relay and I'll do this."

"Hey, wait a minute," protested Dirk. "Shouldn't we try out first?"

Zachary stared at Dirk like he'd suddenly grown a second head. "But you and me are always partners."

"I, uh, just think everyone should have a chance," Dirk said. He cleared his throat and shrugged. "You know, teamwork and all that."

Abby was dumbfounded. "But . . ."

"Fair's fair," said Dana and Dinah at the same time.

"Whatever," sighed Abby. As much as she hated the idea of being paired with either Dirk or Zachary, she wanted the Giggling Grayhounds to win. And that meant using the best person for each event.

She trudged to the finish line. Because it was a backwards obstacle course, the contestants started at the finish line and finished at the starting line. They even had to run backwards. It was hard not to trip over the mats and orange rubber pylons Miss Q had set up.

Melvin gave the signal.

Zachary zipped into the lead, easily dodging every obstacle. He seemed to have eyes in the back of his head. Even though Abby looked over her shoulder to see where she was going, she knocked down three pylons in a row. Dirk wasn't having much luck either. He snagged his heel on a tumbling mat and crashed to the floor. The rest of the Giggling Grayhounds cheered as Zachary crossed the starting line.

Abby groaned. Zachary was obviously the best choice for this event. Which left her and Dirk for the flying saucer relay.

Could this day get any worse?

3 Exciting News

"Mom, we're home," yelled Abby. She slammed the door shut with her foot, then helped Tess struggle out of her backpack.

"Girls?" Mom's voice floated down the hall from her studio at the back of the apartment. That's where the girls usually found her when they got home from school, unless she was giving art classes at the local community center. "Come in here. I've got some great news."

Abby and Tess raced down the hall and arrived at the studio at the same time. Tess, as usual, tried to elbow past Abby to get through the doorway first. With a sigh, Abby stepped back and let her sister pass.

"Woof!" barked Tess. She galloped across the room and leapt on Mom, who was sorting through a new shipment of art supplies. Camel hair brushes and fat tubes of acrylic paint were spread in a circle around her.

"I could use some good news," said Abby.

Especially after a day like today, she thought.

Mom wrapped her arms around Tess and sat cross-legged on the floor. "How does a job sound?" she asked, smiling across the room at Abby.

"A pet-sitting job?" Abby felt her spirits lift. She had started her own pet-sitting business with Tess as her helper. Since their apartment building didn't allow pets, it was the only way she could be around animals. They'd had some pretty unusual experiences. Their last job, when they'd looked after a hamster, had almost ended in disaster. And before that they'd had to take care of a pig that was spoiled rotten.

"A job would be great!" cried Abby. "What kind of pet? When do we start?"

"Whoa," said Mom, laughing. "Slow down. A new teacher at the community center is going away and needs someone to look after her son's pets."

"Pets?" repeated Abby. This was sounding better and better. She made her way through the cluttered room until she was standing directly in front of Mom. "So what kind of animals are they?"

"The job would be for several days," Mom continued as though she hadn't heard the question. She scratched Tess behind one ear and avoided Abby's gaze. "I told her I'd see if you were interested."

"Of course I'm interested," exclaimed Abby. The suspense was driving her crazy. "What kinds of pets do they have?"

Mom hesitated. "Well . . . ants."

Abby stared at her. "You're kidding, right?"

Tess let out a yelp of excitement and sat up straighter on Mom's lap.

"Her son has an ant colony," said Mom. "Of course, it's impossible to take it on the airplane, so they need a pet-sitter."

"Ants," Abby murmured with a shudder. "But you know how I feel about bugs."

"I know you dislike them," Mom said. "But I also know you're a professional. At any rate, it's up to you. I said you'd call."

Abby groaned. "Would I have to touch them?"

"I could teach them tricks," Tess panted, her eyes bright with excitement. "Like in a flea circus!"

"I don't think that would be a good idea," said Mom with a grin. She dug into her pocket and pulled out a scrap of paper. She handed it to Abby with a wink. "They're not the kind of pets you take out for a walk. In fact, I'm pretty sure Margaret would prefer it if you kept the ants in the colony."

Abby took the paper. She looked at Tess's eager face, then at Mom's expectant one. Tess climbed off Mom's lap and sat back on her haunches and whined, like a puppy begging for table scraps.

"Oh, all right," Abby said finally. "Let's do it. I just hope I'm not making a huge mistake."

"Yippee! Yippee!" Tess sang with delight.

Mom beamed at Abby. "Good for you. I knew you wouldn't let an opportunity like this pass you by."

Abby grumbled all the way to the kitchen. She hated bugs, but she knew it would be silly to miss out on a pet-sitting job just because she felt squeamish. Besides, didn't Dad always say that the best way to get rid of your fears was to face them?

Feeling rather proud of herself, she dialed the number Mom had given her. It rang twice, then someone picked up the phone.

"Hello?" answered a squeaky voice.

Abby froze. She recognized that voice. It sounded like someone she knew, someone from school, someone she'd talked to today.

It sounded exactly like Dirk Kaefermann.

4 Abby Takes the Job

"Hello?" demanded Dirk again. "Who's this?"

Abby's first instinct was to slam down the phone, but she forced herself to stay on the line. This is business, she reminded herself grimly.

"Hi. It's Abby. I'm calling about the pet-sitting job."

Dirk gave a laugh that ended in a snort. "Pet-sitting job? Is this some kind of joke?"

"The joke's on you, Dirk," Abby retorted. "Didn't your mom tell you? I'm going to take care of your ants."

"You're making that up," Dirk replied slowly.

"Just put your mom on," Abby sighed.

Dirk didn't answer. A loud noise clattered in Abby's ear and she wondered if he had dropped the phone. "Mom, telephone!" she heard him holler. "It's that weird Abby from my class."

Abby bristled. Weird? If anyone was weird, it was Dirk. He was the one who liked to play with bugs. It didn't surprise her one bit that he had an ant colony instead of a real pet.

Tess came to stand at Abby's elbow, her favorite rubber dog bone clenched between her teeth. She gazed hopefully at her sister.

Abby frowned and pointed at the receiver. "I'm busy," she whispered. "Go away."

Tess pawed at Abby's sleeve and whined, her eyes wide and pleading.

"Shoo," hissed Abby.

Tess's expression drooped behind the rubber bone, then she turned and stomped away. Abby wished she would stop bugging her to play fetch. She felt silly throwing the bone, especially

when they were in front of their apartment building or at the park. Unfortunately, Tess was stubborn. She wouldn't stop until Abby finally got fed up and played along.

"Hello, Abby," said a woman's voice. "Thank you for getting back to me so promptly."

Abby snapped to attention. "Uh, hi. My mom said you might have a pet-sitting job?"

"Yes, that's right. She's been telling me wonderful things about your business, so I immediately thought of you when this trip came up."

Abby was surprised at how nice Mrs. Kaefermann sounded. She didn't seem at all like Dirk. "I have lots of experience," she assured her. "I'd be happy to take the job."

"That's wonderful. On Friday morning we're flying to my sister's wedding and we won't be back until late Monday night. So we'll need a pet-sitter for those four days."

Abby could hear Dirk protesting in the background. She grinned. It was going to drive him nuts that she was in charge of his colony. "No problem," she told Mrs. Kaefermann.

"Did your mother mention the, uh, nature of Dirk's pets?"

"Sure," said Abby as if it were no big deal. "Ants, right?"

"That's right." Mrs. Kaefermann sounded relieved. "Why don't you come home with Dirk after school tomorrow and we'll show you where everything is."

Abby agreed and said goodbye. Maybe this job wouldn't be so bad after all. Mrs. Kaefermann seemed friendly enough. And Dirk would have to be nice to her if he expected her to take good care of his dumb ants. Abby liked that. Plus, she thought, counting the days in her head, he'd be absent until the day before the Crazy Olympics.

But she and Tess still had to walk home with him tomorrow. Dirk already teased her like crazy at school. What would he say when he found out she had a sister who acted like a dog?

5 Not-So-Secret Messages

"Hey, what's that?" Rachel asked the next morning at school, pointing to a piece of paper taped to Abby's coat hook.

Abby shrugged. "I don't know." The paper tore a bit as she pulled it from the hook.

"What does it say?" Rachel leaned closer to get a better look.

"It's just a dumb picture." Abby glared at the paper. "And I know exactly who drew it."

They studied the picture. It was an ant, but not an ordinary one. This was a ferocious killer ant with razor-sharp pincers and fangs that dripped poison. Abby knew it was poison because the artist had drawn a crooked arrow to the dark liquid and written the word "poison" in big letters.

"I don't get it," said Rachel.

Abby crumpled the paper in disgust. "I've got a pet-sitting job taking care of Dirk's ant colony. I don't think he's too happy about it."

"Are the ants really poisonous?" asked Rachel, glancing at the ball of paper in Abby's hand.

"No," scoffed Abby, although she had no idea. "Dirk's just trying to scare me."

"Maybe he likes you," Rachel said with a giggle. "And this is his idea of a love note."

Abby snorted. "Yeah, right." She looked at the crumpled paper again and bit her lip. "Do you really think so?"

Rachel grinned and shrugged. The bell rang and they went into their classroom. As Abby passed Dirk's chair she tossed the scrunched-up note on his desk.

Abby could feel his eyes on the back of her head as she worked on her math equations. She discovered a plastic ant when she dug in her

pencil case for an eraser. Later she found two more drawings of man-eating ants, one on her chair when she returned from sharpening her pencil and another tucked into her science textbook.

Enough is enough, Abby thought. She took the last drawing and used her pink highlighter to give the ant lipstick and a frilly skirt. She tossed it at Dirk when Mrs. Hernandez wasn't looking.

Then it was time for gym.

"If anything happens to my colony, you'll be sorry," Dirk told Abby as they waited under the basketball hoop for the rest of the Giggling Grayhounds.

"Whatever," said Abby.

"I mean it," he insisted. "And don't even think about touching anything in my room."

Abby gave him a withering look.

"We're here," declared Dana. She and Dinah hopped up, already tied together at the knees and ankles. Zachary and Melvin joined them.

"Let's start practicing," cried Zachary. "The Giggling Grayhounds are going to win every event in the Crazy Olympics!"

Melvin nodded, his eyes bright behind his thick glasses.

Abby tried to look enthusiastic, but it was hard. Being on the same team as Dirk was bad enough, but being his relay partner was the absolute worst. She had a sinking feeling it was going to be a disaster.

The four relay teams gathered at one end of the gym, with the Fantastic French Fries first in line. Abby was glad to have a chance to study the race. It looked pretty simple. Rachel and Autumn ran to the other end of the gym, tossing a flat plastic saucer back and forth between them. It was almost like a dance. Step, step, throw. Step, step, catch.

Then it was Abby and Dirk's turn.

They couldn't have done any worse if they'd tried. Abby's throws were wild and Dirk tripped twice trying to catch them. When the whistle blew, Dirk stomped off, red-faced.

"Boy, you guys sure need to practice," Dana told Abby.

"Yeah," added Dinah, shaking her head. "You'll never win like that."

Abby frowned. Everyone knew Dirk was great at sports, so it was obvious who was to blame. If there was one thing Abby hated, it was looking stupid.

Life would be much simpler as a Fantastic French Fry!

6 Left Behind

"Are we going to see the ants now?" asked Tess. She and Abby were standing beside the school flagpole. They always met there before walking home together.

Abby nodded without enthusiasm. "Yeah, we just have to wait for Dirk."

The front of the school was easy to see from where they stood. Abby and Tess watched kids pour through the doors in a steady stream. Dirk was nowhere to be seen.

"So where is he?" Tess asked after a while. By now only a few students were trickling out.

"I don't know. His mom said he'd walk with us," Abby replied. She thought about the ant drawings and the dirty looks Dirk had been shooting her all day. "I bet he ditched us and went home alone."

They waited several more minutes. No Dirk. He must have snuck out a different door, thought Abby angrily.

"Come on," she told Tess. "I know where he lives. It's on our way home."

Tess skipped along beside her sister. "We did sculptures in art," she said. "Mrs. Marino told me my sculpture was stinky-tive. Is that bad?"

Abby tried not to laugh. "She probably said distinctive. That's a good thing. It means your sculpture was different from everybody else's." If there was one thing Tess was good at, it was being distinctive.

Tess barked and looked relieved. "Oh, I thought she meant it was smelly."

Abby smiled, then bit her lip and frowned. What really stunk was being partnered with Dirk in the flying saucer relay. Not to mention the way Dirk had been acting all day. First the nasty notes and now standing her up after school.

They walked another block. Tess bent down and picked up a twig. It was dry and gray, with all the bark rubbed off. "Want to play fetch?"

Abby groaned. Not that again. When Tess got hold of an idea, she never let it go. "Why don't you play by yourself?" she suggested.

"I can't play fetch alone," said Tess, pouting. She held out the stick. "Please?"

"No way." Abby shook her head firmly. She wasn't in the mood to look stupid again. Once a day was enough. "Besides," she added, still thinking of the Crazy Olympics, "sometimes it's better to do things on your own."

Too bad she couldn't compete in an event by herself, she thought. Bowling with cantaloupes looked pretty good to her right now. Instead, she was stuck with the ridiculous flying saucer relay. Nobody could possibly be good at that race. Except someone weird, like Dirk.

Tess growled under her breath. She dragged the stick along a picket fence as they walked. The *clickety, clickety, clickety* of the stick hitting the wooden slats filled the air.

"This is it," Abby said, stopping in front of a square white house with bright red shutters. A tire swing hung from an enormous tree in the

33

front yard. She turned to Tess. "Ready?"

Tess sighed and threw the twig away. She clumped up the front steps and watched Abby ring the doorbell.

A plump woman with short, curly hair and gold hoop earrings opened the door. "Hello girls. I thought you were walking home with Dirk."

So did I, thought Abby. "We must have missed him," she said instead. She didn't like Dirk, but she didn't want to be a tattletale either.

"Hmmmm," said Mrs. Kaefermann with a small frown. She motioned them inside and led them to the kitchen where Dirk sat slouched in a chair, eating a brownie. "Come in and have a snack. Afterwards, Dirk will show you the ants. I'm sure he has all kinds of helpful advice to give you. Isn't that right, Dirk?"

7 Abby Meets the Ants

Dirk was silent. With a small shake of her head, Mrs. Kaefermann turned to Abby. "Would you girls like something to eat?" she asked.

Tess barked happily.

Mrs. Kaefermann looked at her, startled. Abby smiled weakly and stole a glance at Dirk to see if he was paying attention. Luckily, he was still concentrating on his brownie.

"Help yourself." Mrs. Kaefermann gestured to the plate on the table. "Dirk's usually starving when he gets home from school. He must work hard in class."

Abby stifled a snort. The only thing he works hard at is being irritating, she thought to herself.

As if reading her mind, Dirk shoved his chair back from the table, scraping the legs noisily on the linoleum floor. "I'm done," he announced. "I'm going to my room."

"But Abby and Tess haven't . . ." protested

Mrs. Kaefermann.

"That's okay," said Abby quickly. She didn't want to be here any longer than she had to. "Maybe we should go look at the ants now."

Tess gazed longingly at the brownies and started to say something. Abby shot her a warning look. With a sigh, Tess closed her mouth and followed Mrs. Kaefermann out of the room.

"Your mom is very proud of you girls," Mrs. Kaefermann said as they cut through the living room to a short hallway. "She told me about some of your other pet-sitting jobs."

A warm feeling rushed through Abby. Sometimes Mom came home from the community center with funny stories about her art students and the other teachers. It felt kind of nice to know that while she was there she bragged about Abby's pet-sitting business.

"It's hard work sometimes, but I like it," she said.

"We like it," corrected Tess.

At the end of the hall Abby noticed a big sign taped to a door. As they got closer she recognized the ant drawings that decorated it. They were just like the ones Dirk had given her at school, only without the fangs and poison. In the center was the word "Antville."

Mrs. Kaefermann opened the door without knocking. "Enter at your own risk, girls," she said with a slight grimace.

Dirk's mother was friendly and their house seemed normal, but Dirk's bedroom looked exactly as Abby had imagined it would. Like a bomb had gone off.

Blankets and sheets were bunched up in a hill at the foot of the bed. Dirty clothes were piled high on every available surface. The floor was so littered with soccer equipment and books and sneakers that Abby couldn't even see it. Dirk stared at them from the far corner of the room, his shoulders hunched and his hands thrust deep in his pockets.

"Dirk, I asked you to tidy up," said Mrs. Kaefermann, exasperated. She nudged a soiled sweatshirt with her toe.

"Sorry, I forgot," he mumbled. Abby thought he looked embarrassed.

Behind him Abby spotted what must be Antville. It was gigantic. She'd seen ant colonies for sale at the pet store, but they were small plastic containers that fit easily on a shelf or desk. They were nothing like this.

Dirk's colony was a skinny, rectangular structure that stood upright on a low table. It was almost entirely made of glass. The top was fitted with a screened lid and inside it was filled almost to the brim with sand.

Tess bounded across the room and skidded to a stop beside Dirk. She stared at the ant colony, then turned and grinned at Abby. "Cool!"

Abby picked her way through the mess more slowly. It reminded her of Tess's side of their bedroom at home. It was always a complete disaster too.

"Well," said Mrs. Kaefermann uncertainly. "I've still got some packing to do. Dirk will explain everything, won't you Dirk?" She smiled

at her son, but Abby noticed the warning look in her eye. She left the door open behind her.

Abby and Dirk glared at each other, neither one willing to make the first move.

"Boy," piped up Tess. "That's the most stinky-tive bunch of ants I ever saw."

8 Tess Makes a Friend

"Stinky-what?" demanded Dirk.

"She means distinctive," Abby said before Tess could repeat herself. "It's a compliment."

Tess let out a happy bark. "I like your ants," she said with a huge grin.

Dirk stared at her for a moment, then shrugged. "I've had them for a long time," he said. "My Dad built the colony for me last year and we spent the whole summer collecting ants."

"Wow," said Tess. "I bet you have a million of them."

Abby forced herself to look at the colony. A maze of tunnels wound through the sand. Many of them ended in little caves. Dirk had identified several of the caves, labeling them like towns on a road map.

Curious in spite of herself, Abby looked more closely. There really were an awful lot of ants in there. She watched them march around, intent on their business.

"Not a million," said Dirk, although he seemed flattered. "I've tried to count them but they never sit still. And the queen lays tons of eggs."

"The queen?" Tess's eyes lit up. "Where?"

"There," he said, stabbing his finger at the glass. "In her room."

"Where's her crown?" Tess asked, disappointed.

Dirk laughed. "She doesn't wear a crown, but I know she's the queen because she's much bigger than the worker ants. She's the only one who can lay eggs, so she's pretty important."

Tess practically had her nose pressed up against the glass. "Wow," she murmured.

Abby watched the two of them, secretly amazed. This didn't seem like the Dirk she knew. At school he would have made fun of Tess for barking. But here, he was almost . . . nice.

Dirk pointed to a cave near the queen. "That's the nursery," he explained. "The larvae

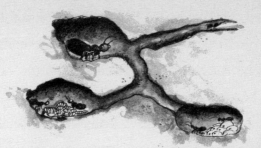

are kept there and worker ants take care of
them. They're kind of like nannies, or babysitters. They do a good job, too. If it's cold the
worker ants move the larvae to the top of the
nest during the day so they can be warm, then
at night they put them back to bed, nice and
cozy. They even wash and feed them. Pretty
cool, huh?"

Tess studied the nursery. "Neat."

"So what am I supposed to do?" Abby
interrupted suddenly.

"We," said Tess. She frowned at her sister.
"I'm your helper, remember?"

"Just feed them," Dirk replied without
looking at her. "And don't wreck anything. Can
you handle that?"

Abby glared at the back of Dirk's head. Just when she was beginning to think he was human, he went and ruined it. "Gee, maybe I should be taking notes," she snapped.

Actually, when Abby had a pet-sitting job, the first thing she usually did was head for the library to do some research. She liked to know everything she could about the animal she would be looking after. But this time she hadn't bothered. They were just a bunch of dumb bugs, after all.

"I heard about some of your other jobs," Dirk said without taking his eyes off the colony. "You'd better not let my ants escape or anything."

Abby thought of Mrs. Nibbles the hamster, who'd gotten lost while exploring in her exercise ball. She wondered how much Mom had told Mrs. Kaefermann. "That won't happen," she scoffed, crossing her fingers behind her back. "I'm a professional."

Dirk turned to Tess. "Do you want to feed them now?"

"Sure," said Tess.

Abby scowled. If Dirk wanted to ignore her, fine. She could care less. He could be Tess's new best friend and it wouldn't bother her one bit.

Dirk pointed to a small sponge at the top of the nest. "Keep this wet at all times," he said. "Ants can survive without food for awhile, but they'll die without water. Make sure you wet it every day, okay?"

Tess's face was grave as she listened intently. "Okay," she promised.

"Did you know that ants can't swallow solid food?" Dirk asked.

Tess shook her head, her eyes wide.

Dirk lowered his voice for effect. "They squeeze the juice out of their food, drink it, then throw away the dry part. And they have two stomachs," he added with relish. "One to hold the food they plan to share and one to digest what they eat. They take the food for sharing home and spit it into the mouths of other ants . . ."

Abby gulped. This was more than she needed to know. Tess, on the other hand, was hanging on every word.

"Come on, I keep their food in the kitchen," Dirk said. He and Tess brushed past Abby.

Abby heard them laughing as they walked down the hall. She looked at Antville. Why had she agreed to take this job?

Because I'm a pet-sitter, she reminded herself. It's good experience. And the money's nice too, she admitted. As much as she hated the idea of running after Dirk, she had a job to do and she needed to know how to do it.

With a sigh, she headed down the hall.

9 Bugsicles!

"I keep their food in the fridge," Dirk was saying as Abby entered the kitchen. He yanked open the refrigerator door and grabbed a small glass bottle from the top shelf. He handed it to Tess. "I make it myself."

"What's in it?" asked Tess. She sniffed the bottle. "It smells yummy!"

Dirk listed the ingredients on his fingers. "Honey and water and vitamins and minerals. Use the eyedropper to give them a few drops every day. And don't forget to put the bottle back in the fridge when you're done. It has to stay cold."

Tess nodded solemnly and crossed her heart with her free hand.

"Ants need a balanced diet," said Dirk as he rummaged in the freezer. He pulled out a plastic container and gave it a shake. It rattled. "They also need protein."

Abby gulped. She remembered Angus, the green anole lizard they'd looked after once. He had needed protein in his diet too, but his protein had turned out to be live crickets.

Ants couldn't eat crickets, could they? Crickets were way bigger than they were. Besides, insects couldn't survive in the freezer. Maybe it was cheese curds or peanuts or . . .

Dirk pried off the lid and shoved the container under Abby's nose. "I collect them myself."

Lying on the bottom of the container were about a dozen chocolate chips. Abby looked more closely. They weren't chocolate chips at all, they were bugs! Icy, shriveled up bugs. Frozen spiders and flies and . . . even crickets.

"Bugsicles," Dirk crowed, flashing Abby a gleeful grin.

"Blech," said Tess.

Inwardly, Abby agreed with Tess, but she refused to let Dirk see her true feelings. "How many do you give them each day?" she asked, pretending to be interested.

Dirk's smile faded. "One or two." He snapped the lid back on the container.

"Okay," said Abby with a shrug. "Let's get going."

Dirk carried the bugsicles to his room. He showed the girls how to open the screened lid, then let Tess squirt two drops of honey mixture onto a small aluminum plate. Abby was relieved when he popped a frozen bug into the colony himself instead of offering the container to her.

"That's it," he said. He made sure the lid to the colony was firmly in place, then left to put the food back in the fridge.

"This won't be hard," said Abby. "It's not so bad when the bugs are frozen."

Tess barked agreeably. She prowled around the room, stopping to sniff a model volcano made of clay.

"Dirk's pets are kind of interesting," Abby added, surprising herself. Already a few ants had found the food, sucked it into their first stomach, and started back down the tunnels. "I mean, they're still gross to look at," she said, watching them march in single file. "But they must be pretty smart if they have nurseries and stuff. Don't you think?"

Squeak, squeak. Squeak, squeak.

Abby whirled around to see Tess bouncing up and down on Dirk's bed. She had something flat and round clamped between her teeth.

"What are you doing?" hissed Abby, glancing at the door. Dirk would be back any second. "Spit that out!"

Tess jumped off the bed and landed beside Abby. She growled playfully, shaking her head back and forth so that her ponytails flapped in her eyes. Only then did Abby realize what Tess had in her mouth.

A saucer.

And not any ordinary saucer, either. This one was midnight blue with silver lightning bolts that flashed in the light. The words "Super Sonic Saucer" were written across it.

Abby grabbed the saucer and wrestled it from Tess's mouth. Her fingers tingled. There was something special about this saucer. She had the feeling that if she threw it, it would go exactly where she wanted it to.

"What are you doing?"

Startled, Abby dropped the Super Sonic on the floor. Dirk stood in the doorway, glaring at her. "I'm sorry," she stammered. "Tess was . . ."

"Zachary told me you'd be snoopy," Dirk said. He marched over, picked up the saucer and waved it in her face. "I meant what I said before. Hands off my stuff, or else."

"Fine," snapped Abby. Like she'd even want to touch any of his stupid stuff! Grabbing Tess by the arm, she stomped out of his bedroom without looking back.

10 Flying Solo

"Wake up, girls," called Mom. "Breakfast is ready."

Abby opened her eyes and felt happier than she had in a long time. Today was Friday, the day Dirk was flying to his aunt's wedding. He wouldn't be at school to make her look stupid in gym class and he wouldn't be at home to bother her while she took care of her pet-sitting duties.

A Dirk-free day!

"Wake up, Tess," she called to the lump in the bed across the room. Humming, Abby flung back the covers and scrambled into her clothes.

The lump moaned, but didn't move.

Abby slid on her favorite purple bead anklet, then grabbed her key string from the bedpost and slipped it over her head. She was proud that her parents had agreed she was old enough to have her own apartment key. She couldn't wait to add Mrs. Kaefermann's key to the string.

Tess poked her head out of her blankets and blinked.

"Morning," Abby greeted her cheerfully.

"Why are you so happy?" mumbled Tess.

"Lots of reasons," Abby replied. "For one thing, I'm getting paid to squirt sugar water into a box of bugs. Talk about easy money. And best of all, Dirk is gone."

Tess struggled to sit up. "Why does that make you happy?"

"Never mind. Just hurry up and get dressed," Abby said. "Today's my lucky day and I don't want to waste a minute of it."

School was great. Nobody left notes in her textbooks. Nobody bumped into her desk when she was writing in her journal. And nobody broke the tip on her pencil every time she left her seat.

Abby practically skipped down the hall to gym class. The Giggling Grayhounds were gathered in their spot under the basketball hoop. Only today they were one member short.

"We've got three more school days until the Olympics," Zachary told the group. "We need to practice, practice, practice."

"How can Abby practice without a partner?" asked Dana.

"I don't need a partner," Abby assured them. "I'll just work on my technique."

Dinah looked skeptical. "Alone?"

"Sure," said Abby. "I'm much better on my own. Dirk's not all that great, you know."

Zachary snorted. "Are you kidding? Dirk's the champ! He even got a Super Sonic for his birthday. Those things are amazing."

Abby remembered the midnight blue saucer in Dirk's room. She'd be a champ too with a saucer like that. Her thoughts were interrupted by a blast from Miss Q's whistle.

It was time to begin.

Abby selected a saucer and curled her fingers lightly around its smooth edge. The Super Sonic had felt so much better in her hand. Taking a deep breath, she aimed at a spot on the gym wall and let it fly.

She missed the mark completely.

She tried again. And again. It was like the saucer had a mind of its own. Could it be warped or something?

"I'll practice with you," offered Melvin.

"I don't need to practice," she said, glaring at him. "I need a new saucer. This one's defective."

Melvin's shoulders sagged. He started to walk away.

"Wait," said Abby. She hated to make Melvin feel bad. He never teased her like Dirk did. "Come back. Maybe I could use some help."

They tossed the saucer back and forth a few times, but it was like there was a force field around Melvin. No matter how carefully she aimed, Abby couldn't get the saucer to his outstretched hands. It either veered away or flew right over his head.

"I need a break," she finally said. She sank to the floor and leaned against the wall. Melvin retrieved the saucer and sat beside her.

"You're getting better," he said.

Feeling miserable, Abby shook her head. "We're going to lose. And it'll be all my fault."

"You just need more practice," Melvin told her. He pushed his glasses further up the bridge of his nose. "Besides, it's a team effort. Nobody wins or loses a relay all by themselves."

Abby stared at the floor. She didn't want to hurt Melvin's feelings, but she knew the Crazy Olympics were going to be awful. She could practice until she was blue in the face and she still wouldn't be any good. Everybody would laugh at her. And she knew Dirk would be laughing loudest of all.

11 Abby Takes Control

Abby was still in a bad mood when she and Tess headed for Dirk's house after school. What had Melvin said? Something about nobody being able to win a relay all by themselves. She muttered the words under her breath as she trudged along.

They seemed familiar. Hadn't Tess complained about not being able to play fetch all by herself? She'd been pretty upset when Abby had refused to throw her the bone.

Maybe Tess and Melvin had a point.

It was true that she liked doing stuff on her own. But so what? Working as part of a team meant depending on someone else, and that wasn't always a good idea. Especially if you wanted things to turn out.

"Can I feed the ants today?" asked Tess.

"I'd better do it," Abby said. "If anything happens to Dirk's precious bugs, he'll have a fit."

"That's not fair," protested Tess. "You

never let me do anything! I'm supposed to be your helper, remember?"

Abby shrugged. "Sorry Tess, but I have no choice. Dirk is just waiting for me to screw up."

Mrs. Kaefermann had taped the house key to the bottom of the mailbox. Abby unlocked the door and slipped the key onto the string around her neck. The usual thrill wasn't there. Having a second key on her string wasn't much fun if the job only brought trouble.

She went straight to the kitchen to get the honey mixture and the bugsicles. Then she rummaged through the kitchen drawers until she found a spoon. There was no way she was going to touch a frozen bug.

Tess trailed along behind her as they made their way to Dirk's room. His door was closed and there was a yellow note stuck to it.

"*Do Not Enter!!*" it read.

"What does it say?" asked Tess.

"Nothing. Just one of Dirk's dumb ideas." Abby pushed the door open. There were yellow sticky notes everywhere — on his dresser drawers, his reading lamp, and even his airplane mobile.

"*Stay out! Don't touch! Off limits!*" they warned.

"Is he mad at us?" asked Tess, staring around the room.

"That's just the way he is," Abby said with disgust. "Rachel's nuts if she thinks he likes me. She got it right the first time . . . Dirk is a jerk."

Tess looked confused. "I think he's nice."

Abby rolled her eyes. Dirk? Nice?

Ignoring the messages, she walked over to Antville. She didn't want the bugsicles to melt. The first thing she noticed was a yellow note stuck to the glass.

"*Feed Us!*" it said.

Abby scowled. She crumpled up the note and tossed it into the garbage can. How dumb did he think she was?

The bugsicles rattled in their container as she pried off the lid. Using the spoon, she selected two hard lumps. They looked like houseflies. She removed the screen at the top of the colony and dropped the frozen insects onto the sand.

They bounced, then rolled to a stop.

Abby set the bugsicle container aside. That hadn't been so bad. She squirted a few drops of honey mixture onto the aluminum plate and removed the sponge. This job was going to be a cinch.

Tess followed her to the bathroom. She rested her chin on the countertop and watched her sister work. Abby rinsed the sand off the sponge, squeezing it several times as the water flowed over it. Then she let it get soaking wet. Back in Dirk's room, Abby placed the sponge on the sand and secured the lid.

"All done," she said, checking her watch. "And it only took fifteen minutes. What an easy job."

Tess growled and stomped away.

Abby opened her mouth to say something, but closed it again. She knew Tess didn't like being left out, but if anything happened to Antville, Dirk would never let her forget it.

This was one job Abby needed to do by herself.

12 A Research Expedition

The ants were fed and watered, but for some reason Abby felt reluctant to leave.

Good pet-sitters do more than feed the pets, she told herself. They make sure they're happy and healthy too. She peered through the glass at the nursery, but she wasn't sure what to look for. What was normal in an ant colony?

Her gaze fell on a spiral notebook that was lying on the table beside the colony. It was an ordinary notebook with a yellow piece of paper stuck to the cover.

Another note from Dirk.

It read, "*Do not open, or else! This means you!!*"

"Are you coming?" Tess stood in the doorway with her arms crossed, but her expression changed when she saw Abby pick up the notebook. "What's that?"

"I don't know," said Abby. "But Dirk sure doesn't want me to look at it."

Tess came to stand beside Abby. She struggled to read what was scrawled across the book's cover. "Myr . . . myrem . . . what does it say?"

The word was long and unfamiliar. "My-re-me-co-logy," Abby read slowly. She'd have to look it up when she got home, but she was almost certain it had something to do with ants. Maybe Dirk kept notes on his pets. That would be valuable information for a pet-sitter. She glanced at the warning one last time, then flipped open the book.

On the first page Dirk had drawn a cartoon ant. It had bulging muscles and wore a superhero cape.

"Super Ant!" Abby read out loud. "Ants can carry ten to fifty times their body weight. This would be like a hundred-pound boy climbing the world's tallest mountain with a small car on his back."

Tess looked at the ant colony. "I don't see any capes," she said with a frown.

The second page showed a diagram of an

ant with all its parts marked and labeled. On the label next to the mouth Dirk had written "*Jaws move sideways, like scissors.*" On the label next to the antennae it said, "*Organ of smell, touch, taste and hearing.*" And on the one near the rear end it said, "*Metasoma, often containing poison sac or stingers.*"

Abby was amazed. She couldn't believe Dirk had done so much research. She'd never thought of him as scientific. Was it possible they actually had something in common?

Reading on, she was surprised to learn that ants were very social creatures. They didn't just scurry around aimlessly, they worked together to keep the colony running smoothly. Every ant had a job. Some workers grew underground fungus farms for food. Others raised insects called aphids to "milk" them of their nectar. There were ants in charge of gathering food, guarding the queen, and even taking out the garbage.

Abby looked at Antville with new respect. Maybe she'd do some research of her own when she got home. It looked like ants weren't so dumb after all.

"It's time to go," she told Tess, snapping the notebook shut.

But the bedroom was empty.

Where was Tess? Abby grabbed the ant food and ran out of the room, calling her sister's name. Please don't let her be wrecking anything, Abby prayed.

"Woof, woof!"

Abby raced through the living room toward the sound. No Tess. She ran into the kitchen. Tess wasn't there either, but the front door was wide open. Quickly, Abby shoved the ant food into the fridge and freezer and ran outside.

Sure enough, Tess was in the front yard. Down on all fours, she was scampering across the grass with something in her mouth. Sunshine glinted off the silver lightning bolts.

"Dirk's saucer," gasped Abby.

Tess twisted her neck sideways and tried to fling the saucer into the air. It dropped next to her hands. She barked, picked it up in her teeth, and tried again. This time the saucer landed on its side and wobbled a few times before it fell. Abby ran across the lawn and snatched it up.

"Are you crazy?" she sputtered. "Dirk will kill me if you wreck his saucer."

Tess sat back on her haunches. "I'm bored. You won't let me help with Antville and you won't play fetch with me." Her voice began to waver. "So I'm playing by myself."

Abby didn't know what to say. Tess was her helper, after all. But this job was different from the others. Dirk would have a fit if he found out they'd messed around with his stuff.

"If I let you feed the ants tomorrow, will you promise not to touch anything else?" she asked.

Tess sniffed back a tear. "I promise."

"Fine," Abby said, softening at her sister's hangdog expression. It was impossible to stay mad at Tess for long. "Wait here while I put this back. Then we'll go home, okay?"

Abby walked back into the house, inspecting the saucer. She was relieved to see that Tess hadn't scratched it. All she had to do was put it back exactly where Dirk had left it and everything would be fine.

When she got to the hallway, Abby hesitated. The Super Sonic felt so good in her hand. She held it the way she would if she were going to toss it to someone. She stretched out her arm, then curled it back toward her body. It had beautiful balance. She wished she could throw it, just once. She was certain it would glide through the air in a perfect arc . . .

Suddenly her fingers slipped.

Abby watched in horror as the Super Sonic Saucer flew down the hall, across Dirk's room and straight for Antville.

13 Earthquake!

"Noooo," cried Abby, but it was too late.

The saucer ricocheted off the front of the ant colony and disappeared under Dirk's bed. She held her breath. The glass rattled, the wood shuddered, but the colony didn't tip over.

Abby exhaled slowly. That was a close call. Too close. What if Antville had crashed to the floor and shattered into a million pieces? The ants would have escaped and it would have been impossible to rescue them all.

"Everything's okay," she whispered. "Antville is fine and the Super Sonic is fine and Dirk will never know this happened."

Still, her legs wobbled as she walked over

to the ant colony. Thank goodness it was big and heavy. A smaller colony would have been knocked over for sure. She touched the spot where the saucer had slammed into it, glad to see there were no cracks in the glass.

Then she noticed the damage.

Everything wasn't okay. The area where the saucer had hit was a disaster zone. Many of the tunnels had collapsed and some of the chambers had caved in. Abby imagined she could see terror on the ant's faces as they struggled to move through the sand.

"The nursery," she cried. Her knees trembled as she searched for the special room that held the larvae. The nursery had crumbled. The babies were buried under a thousand grains of sand!

Tess ran into the room. "What's taking you so long?" she asked. "I thought we were going home." She stopped and stared at Abby. "Are you okay?"

"I killed them," moaned Abby. "It's all my fault."

Tess turned to Antville and gasped. "Was there an earthquake?"

Abby sank down on the carpet, covering her face with her hands. "I didn't mean to throw the saucer, it just sort of happened. Now all the baby ants are dead. Everything is ruined. I'm a terrible pet-sitter."

Tess put her arm around Abby's shoulders. "It was an accident," she said softly. "I'll tell Dirk what happened. He'll understand."

Abby turned her face away. She knew Dirk would never understand. He'd have every right to hate her. All she'd had to do was feed the ants, and instead she'd destroyed a whole generation of them.

"Abby," cried Tess. She pointed at the ruined colony. "Look!"

Abby shook her head. Tears slid down her cheeks. She thought of the tiny, helpless larvae, crushed by the sand. It was too awful.

"They're not dead!" Tess insisted. "They called 911!"

Abby stared at her sister. "What are you

talking about?"

Tess pointed at Antville. "Just look!"

Dreading what she might see, Abby faced the colony. At first it seemed the same. But then, with a gasp, she noticed that something was happening.

Tess was right!

Already, dozens of worker ants were digging through the collapsed tunnels, using their saliva to repair the damaged walls. One by one, they were rescuing the larvae and carrying them to safety.

Abby had never seen anything like it. Instead of sticking to their usual jobs, the ants were working together like one gigantic relay team. They weren't arguing over who was the strongest or the fastest. The babysitters, the garbage collectors . . . they were all pulling together to save the babies and rebuild the colony.

If the Giggling Grayhounds worked that well together, Abby thought, we'd win the Crazy Olympics for sure.

She wiped the tears from her cheeks. The larvae were safe. She wasn't a murderer after all.

Then she thought of Dirk. Would the colony be back to normal by the time he came home?

Race Against Time

Abby tossed and turned all night. She woke the next morning, bleary-eyed and worried. Would the ants really be able to repair all the damage before Dirk came home?

She went over and over the terrible accident in her mind. All through breakfast she remembered how the Super Sonic had hurtled toward Antville. While she brushed her teeth she pictured the collapsed tunnels and caves. She tried to watch the Saturday morning cartoons with Tess, but all she could think about was the ruined nursery.

Finally Abby couldn't stand it any longer. "I've got to go check on Antville," she said, heading for the door. "You can finish watching cartoons if you want."

Tess leapt off the couch and ran after her. "Wait for me!"

When they got to Dirk's house Abby rushed straight to his bedroom, desperate to see what the ants had accomplished overnight.

"There's the larvae," she cried, pointing at a newly dug chamber.

"And the queen," Tess added, spotting her nearby.

A few of the smaller side tunnels still lay in ruins, but it was business as usual everywhere else. Some of the ants were working on the tunnels, some were busy making new caves, and some were digging out food from the collapsed storage rooms.

Abby admired all the new construction. "You guys must have worked all night," she said. "Lucky for me."

Then she looked at Dirk's labels. Many of them were now in the wrong place. Carefully, she peeled off the one that said "Nursery" and placed it near the larvae's new living quarters. She hoped Dirk wouldn't notice.

While Tess was busy watching the activity, Abby ran for the food. She felt like she'd been given a second chance and this time she was going to make sure everything went perfectly.

Not bothering with a spoon, she chose three frozen lumps at random and dropped them into the nest. She gave the ants two drops of the honey mixture, then squirted out a couple more. They could probably use the extra energy.

"Hey," protested Tess, tearing herself away from the glass. "You said I could help today."

Abby groaned. She had forgotten her promise. "Why don't you do the water," she said at last. "Remember how important Dirk said that was? And just think how thirsty you'd be if you had to rebuild our entire apartment."

Tess growled under her breath, but stood on her tiptoes and reached for the sponge. She disappeared into the bathroom, returning a few moments later. Her forehead wrinkled with concentration as she put the wet sponge back into the nest.

Abby replaced the screened lid, but first she poked the sponge with one finger. She caught Tess watching her.

"Don't you trust me?" asked Tess, frowning.

"Of course," Abby assured her. "I just wanted to double check, that's all."

"Hrumph," grunted Tess.

Abby gathered up the food containers to take them back to the kitchen. Dirk's notebook was lying on the table. She bit her lip, then tucked it inside her shirt when Tess wasn't looking. If the ants were giving her a second chance, the least she could do was learn everything she could about them. The notebook was full of important information.

It's not stealing, she told herself, not if I bring it back first thing tomorrow morning.

Abby woke up early the next morning, turning off her alarm before it rang. She tiptoed over to her sister's bed. "Wake up," she whispered. Tess groaned and pulled the covers over her head.

"Come on," Abby tried again. She was answered with a soft snore. Giving up, she dressed quickly and slipped her key string around her neck. She felt under her pillow for Dirk's notebook. It had to be returned today,

and if Tess wasn't there to see her put it back, all the better.

"Good morning," said Mom when Abby walked into the kitchen. "You look like you slept better last night."

"Yeah, I guess so," said Abby.

"How's the job going?" Dad asked.

"It's more complicated than I expected," she answered slowly, thinking of the earthquake. "But I can handle it."

Dad smiled. "You're not grossed out by the ants?"

"They're not so bad." She helped herself to a piece of toast. "Ants are very civilized. Did you know that of all the insects in the world, ants have the largest brains? It's estimated that an ant's brain may have the same processing power as a computer."

"Sounds like you did your homework," chuckled Dad. "As usual."

Dirk's notebook suddenly felt heavy in her hand. She hoped her parents wouldn't ask about it. "Yeah, I guess. Well . . . I'd better go feed them. I'll see you later," she said, edging toward the hall.

"Wait," called Mom. "Aren't you taking Tess with you?"

"I tried." Abby shrugged. "But she won't get up. You know how she is in the morning. She'll probably still be sleeping when I get back."

Mom frowned. "I'm not sure . . ."

"I'll be back before you know it," Abby

said quickly. She kissed Dad on the forehead and practically flew out of the apartment. She ran down the stairs two at a time, then let herself out of the building. It was a relief to feel the fresh air on her face.

Abby hugged the notebook to her chest and watched her feet as she trudged along the sidewalk. She realized Tess wouldn't be happy about being left behind. But what was she supposed to do, pour a pail of water over her head?

Deep down, she knew her attempt to wake Tess had been half-hearted. Frowning, she brushed the thought aside. This job wasn't going very well and she couldn't wait around all morning. She needed to see how the ants were doing. And she needed to put the notebook back before anyone found out she'd taken it.

Reading Dirk's journal last night had made her realize how important his ants were to him. She hated the way he bugged her at school, and his sticky notes were insulting. Still, his mom had hired her to do a job, and he deserved to come home to a happy, healthy colony.

Abby clutched the notebook tighter. Her reputation as a pet-sitter was at stake. If Dirk found out about the earthquake, the whole school would know. Probably even the whole town.

She'd never pet-sit again!

15 Things Start Looking Up

"You guys are amazing," Abby whispered to the busy insects. "Look at what you've done in just a few days." Aside from some of the smaller tunnels, Antville was nearly back to normal.

This time she chose a nice big cricket for their breakfast, dropping it into the colony beside the aluminum plate. Then she squeezed out a few extra drops of the honey mixture. She rinsed and soaked the sponge and closed the screen lid tightly.

"Just keep it up," she told the ants, "and Dirk will never know the difference."

"He will if I tell him."

Abby spun around. "Tess," she cried, "what are you doing here?"

"Mom drove me," growled Tess. There was nothing puppy-doggish about her now. She looked more like an angry pit bull.

"I tried to wake you up . . ." said Abby, letting her words trail off as Tess continued to glare at her.

"You didn't want me here," Tess said. Her anger faded and she looked sad. "You always want to do everything yourself. I could tattle, you know. Then Dirk would tell everyone what a bad pet-sitter you are."

Abby stared at her. "You'd do that?"

Tess scratched behind her left ear, something she always did when she felt confused. "No," she said finally, "but I don't want to be your helper anymore. I quit."

"What?" Abby couldn't believe her ears. Tess loved being her helper.

"You like to do everything by yourself," Tess said, her bottom lip trembling. "So do it. All alone, just the way you like it."

Abby didn't know what to say. Sure, there had been times when she'd wished she had the pet-sitting business all to herself. Taking care of other people's pets had been her idea, after all. But now that Tess was quitting, she didn't feel good at all. She felt guilty, like she'd let Tess down.

She looked at the ants. They continued to

work together to rebuild their community, something a single ant could never have done alone. They'd achieved so much by working as a team.

"You can't quit," she told Tess.

Tess blinked back tears, swiping at her nose with the back of her hand. "Why not?"

"Because," Abby hesitated. She knew what she had to say. Why was it so hard? "Because I need you," she finally admitted.

"Really?" Tess looked uncertain. "Why?"

"We're a team, Tess," she said. "We help each other. Without you, I'd never have known how to take care of the ants. You're the one Dirk gave all the instructions to, right? He wouldn't have told me that stuff in a million years."

"I guess so," said Tess slowly.

"It's all Dirk's fault," Abby said, suddenly angry. "I never would have hogged this job if those ants belonged to someone else. I just kept thinking about what he'd say if something went wrong. He's got such a big mouth."

Tess titled her head to one side. "Huh?"

"I was so worried about him that I forgot

about you. Please don't quit. Having you as my partner is more important to me than what Dirk might blab to everyone."

As Abby held out her fist, pinky finger extended, she made a silent promise to herself to stop being so stubborn. She'd let Tess help more, even if she goofed up now and then. They were sisters, after all. "Just say you'll still be my helper."

Tess hesitated, then hooked pinkies with Abby. She giggled as they did their secret hand-shake, up and down twice, followed by a finger snap. "Okay," she said, happy again. She looked at Antville. "What can I do?"

Abby gulped. She'd already done every-thing. How could she show Tess she was sin-cere? Then she had an idea. Without another word Abby dropped to the floor. Her head and shoulders disappeared under Dirk's bed. When she wriggled out she had something blue and silver in her hand.

"Want to play fetch?" she asked, holding the Super Sonic in the air. "If I don't get better at throwing and catching, Dirk and I will lose

the relay for sure." Abby looked at Tess, feeling like a weight had been lifted from her chest. It hadn't been so hard asking for help after all. It actually felt kind of good.

Tess yipped excitedly and raced for the door.

They played together for an hour. Abby threw the saucer and Tess brought it back in her teeth, like a dog playing in the park with its master. At first Abby's throws landed all over the yard. But gradually her aim improved and the saucer landed closer and closer to Tess. Sometimes too close.

"Ouch," yelped Tess, rubbing her eyebrow. "I think you're getting better."

"Oops, sorry," Abby grinned. The saucer was starting to go where she wanted it to. Maybe she wouldn't embarrass herself after all. If practicing with Tess improved her aim, then maybe practicing with an expert thrower would improve her catching skills.

And everyone knew that Dirk was the champ!

16 D-Day

On Monday during gym Melvin helped Abby work on her technique. She practiced again with Tess at Dirk's house after feeding the ants.

Then it was Tuesday. D-day. D for Dirk, who would be at school any minute. Abby stood in front of his coat hook, biting her lip and scanning the crowd for his mop of red hair. She knew she was doing the right thing, so why did she feel so nervous? What was the worst that could happen?

Finally she spotted Dirk at the end of the hall. She watched him saunter toward her, his dirty blue knapsack slung over one shoulder. Thank goodness he was alone. She wasn't sure she could do this in front of his friends.

"Move it, Captain Loser," Dirk said loudly when he noticed her. He yanked a tattered binder out of his knapsack, then elbowed her aside to hang the bag on his hook.

Abby took a deep breath and counted to three. She reminded herself that he'd never practice with her if she lost her temper. Struggling to keep her voice pleasant, she said, "How was the wedding?"

Dirk stared at her. "Boring."

Abby shifted from one foot to the other and tried again. "Were your ants okay when you got home?"

"Yeah." Dirk nodded. He hesitated, then said, "I guess you must have taken pretty good care of them. They built a whole bunch of new tunnels."

"They were busy," Abby agreed, feeling her cheeks go hot as she thought of the earthquake. She spoke quickly, before she could lose her nerve. "Listen, tomorrow's the Crazy Olympics and I was wondering if you wanted to practice after school with me. I mean, I know I wasn't very good when we tried it before, but I've been working on my throwing and I think we could do better if we gave it another shot."

"Uh . . . yeah, sure." Dirk glanced around

to see if any of his friends were listening.

"Okay," said Abby. "I'll meet you after school by the flagpole." Without waiting for an answer she ran into the classroom.

"Why were you talking to Dirk the jerk?" Rachel whispered, joining Abby at her desk. "Did he give you another one of those dumb notes?"

Abby sat down and opened her journal. "Nope, we were just talking."

"I thought you didn't like him."

"I don't," said Abby. Rachel narrowed her eyes and Abby shifted in her seat. "I mean, he's okay. We're relay partners, that's all. Quit staring at me."

"Sure, whatever," said Rachel with a wink.

Abby was glad when the bell rang and Mrs. Hernandez walked into the room.

Dirk acted differently toward Abby that day. He wasn't exactly nice to her, but he didn't go out of his way to be mean, either. Abby wasn't sure if this was because she'd kept his ants alive or because she'd been friendly to him. Whatever the reason, it was a nice change.

After school she found Tess in their usual spot beside the flagpole. "We're meeting Dirk," she said, waving a saucer she'd borrowed from the gym. "I asked him to practice with me."

Tess cocked her head to one side. "Do you think he'll show up this time?"

Abby shrugged. "I hope so."

Once again they watched as kids poured out the front doors of the school. Abby heard Zachary's familiar high-pitched giggle and caught sight of him whispering something into Jason's ear. Snickering at their private joke, they walked past Abby and Tess without glancing their way. Dirk wasn't with them.

Finally the heavy metal doors slammed shut and stayed that way. Only teachers were left in the building. Abby had to admit that she'd been stood up. Again. Dirk was probably halfway home by now.

She didn't know why she felt so disappointed. She hadn't expected him to be her best friend or anything. But she'd thought they could at least be nice to each other. They had a common goal, didn't they? They both wanted to win the relay. It hadn't been easy asking him for help, the least he could have done was keep his word. What a jerk.

"Come on, Tess," she muttered, feeling like a fool. "Let's go home."

"I'll practice with you," Tess offered. "We can play fetch."

Abby looked at the yellow bruise above Tess's eyebrow and managed a smile. "Okay. But maybe you could try catching the saucer this time, okay?"

"Woof!" barked Tess.

They were almost to the soccer field when Abby heard someone shouting her name.

"Hey, wait up," cried Dirk, running toward them. He had his Super Sonic in one hand and an envelope in the other.

"I went home first," he said, trying to catch his breath. "I thought we could practice with my saucer. It's the best. Maybe we could use it tomorrow in the Olympics. Oh, and my mom wanted me to give you this."

Abby took the envelope. Inside were several coins and a couple of bills folded in half. "Thanks," she said, stuffing the envelope into her backpack. She looked at the Super Sonic, then at Dirk.

"I'm glad you want to practice with me," he said. The tips of his ears grew pink. "I always thought you hated me."

"I don't hate you," Abby replied. "I just

don't like being bugged all the time, you know?"

"Yeah, well, I don't like being called Dirk the jerk, either." Dirk stared at the ground, then dug the toe of his shoe into the grass.

"How about a truce," Abby suggested. "After all, we're on the same team, right?"

"Aye, aye, Captain," he teased, but this time the phrase didn't sting. He looked up at her and held out his saucer. "Truce."

Abby grinned and took the Super Sonic. All of a sudden she wasn't worried about how they would place in the Crazy Olympics. Win or lose, at least she'd know she'd given it her best try. Besides, now that she and Dirk were working together, the Giggling Grayhounds would be hard to beat!

Tess barked impatiently. "Enough talking," she cried. "Let's play fetch!"

"Fetch?" repeated Dirk, giving Abby a puzzled look.

Abby drew back her arm and let the Super Sonic whiz through the air. "Yeah," she said with a laugh, "but don't worry, she doesn't leave teeth marks!"